Corinthians 13:4 Love is patient; love is kind.

**Dedicated to James Pentaudi
who has given so many people
in Gansevoort, NY
a beautiful gift of love.**

James was sitting outside one day,
when Tracy drove up and said, "Hey!".

1

Tracy said, "I've been looking for a church so I can preach about God's good works."

Tracy said, "This is a beautiful old church you have here.", James said, "Come, pull up a chair."

Then James said, "That would be really nice.",
Tracy said, "Awesome! What is your price?"

James said, "There's no price to preach here,
I can see in your eyes that you really do care."

Tracy said, "I will paint and clean and make God's house look nice, that is how I will pay my price."

6

James and Tracy shook hands,
"Because this was all a part of God's plans."

7

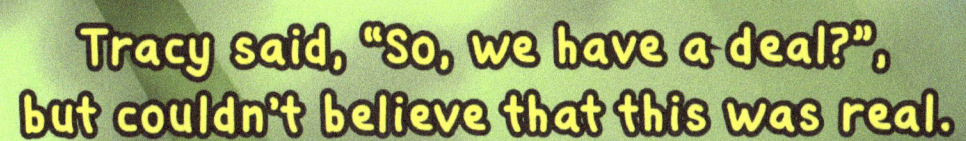

Tracy said, "So, we have a deal?",
but couldn't believe that this was real.

"Now there's a place for the children to come,
to learn about God's word, and have lots of fun!"

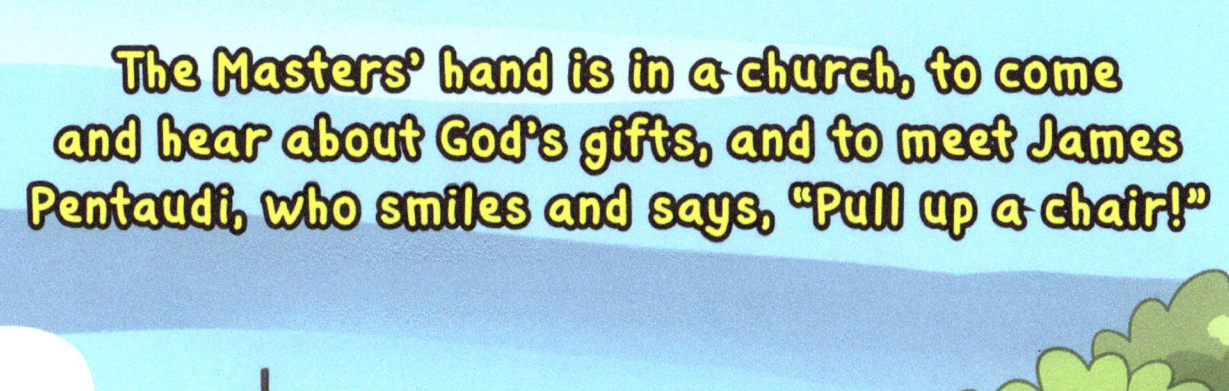

The Masters' hand is in a church, to come
and hear about God's gifts, and to meet James
Pentaudi, who smiles and says, "Pull up a chair!"

Master's Hands

10

John 3:16 For God so loved the world
that he gave his only Son that whoever believes
in Him shall not perish, but shall go to live
in heaven with Him forever.

www.ingramcontent.com/pod-product-compliance
Lightning Source LLC
Chambersburg PA
CBHW041205100726
47911CB00016B/866